Published in North America by Free Spirit Publishing Inc., Minneapolis, Minnesota, 2017

**Library of Congress Cataloging-in-Publication Data**
Names: Barnham, Kay, author. | Gordon, Mike, 1948 March 16– illustrator.
Title: Feeling sad! / written by Kay Barnham ; illustrated by Mike Gordon.
Description: Minneapolis, Minnesota : Free Spirit Publishing Inc., 2017. | Series: Everyday Feelings
Identifiers: LCCN 2017008393| ISBN 9781631982538 (hardcover) | ISBN 1631982532 (hardcover)
Subjects: LCSH: Sadness in children—Juvenile literature. | Sadness—Juvenile literature.
Classification: LCC BF723.S15 B37 2017 | DDC 155.4/124—dc23 LC record available at https://lccn.loc.gov/2017008393

Free Spirit Publishing does not have control over or assume responsibility for author or third-party websites and their content.

Reading Level Grade 2; Interest Level Ages 5–9; Fountas & Pinnell Guided Reading Level M

10 9 8 7 6 5 4 3 2 1
Printed in China
H13660517

**Free Spirit Publishing Inc.**
6325 Sandburg Road, Suite 100
Minneapolis, MN 55427-3674
(612) 338-2068
help4kids@freespirit.com
www.freespirit.com

First published in 2017 by Wayland, a division of Hachette Children's Books · London, UK, and Sydney, Australia
Text © Wayland 2017
Illustrations © Mike Gordon 2017

The rights of Kay Barnham to be identified as the author and Mike Gordon as the illustrator of this Work have been asserted in accordance with the Copyright, Designs and Patents Act, 1988.

Managing editor: Victoria Brooker
Creative design: Paul Cherrill

# feeling SAD!

Written by
Kay Barnham

Illustrated by
Mike Gordon

free spirit
PUBLISHING®

Rio watched as Markus kicked a
soccer ball against the school wall.
He looked really miserable.
"What's wrong with Markus?"
Rio asked Jack.

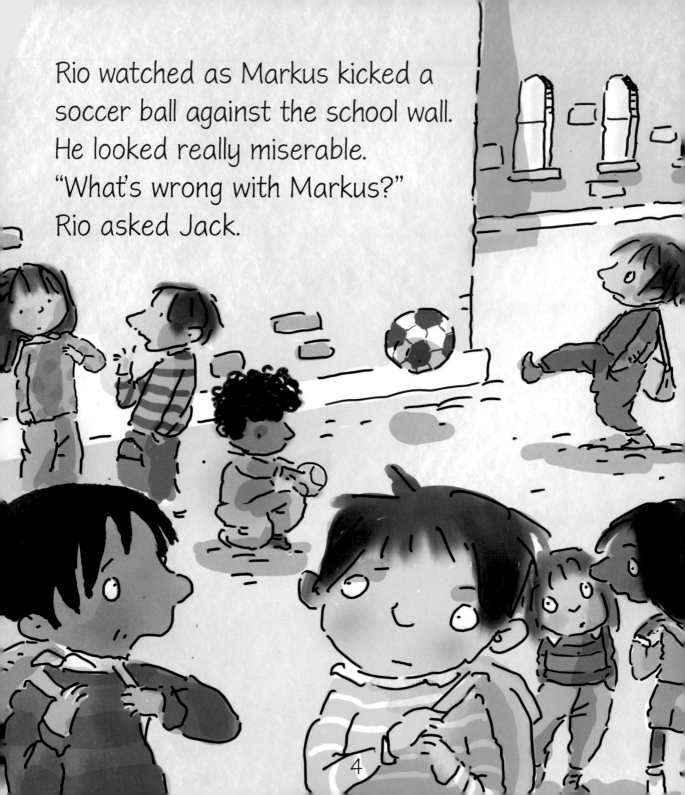

"Haven't you heard?" said Jack.
"He's moving, which means he's changing
schools. He's really upset about it."
"Oh dear," said Rio, who liked Markus a lot.
He decided to try and cheer him up.

Next time the ball headed in Rio's
direction, he kicked it back to Markus.
"Hey," Rio said, "I'm sorry to hear
that you're leaving."

"Not as sorry as I am," mumbled Markus. And he kicked the ball so hard that it flew right over the wall.

"Is there a soccer team at your new school?" asked Rio. Markus brightened a little. "Yeah, I think so."

"That might be a good way to make friends," said Rio.

"Maybe," said Markus. Then his face fell.
"But what if I'm not good enough?"
"You're a *great* player!" said Rio.
"Thanks!" said Markus. He blushed.
"I'll just go and get the ball…"

At lunchtime, Rio heard an odd noise in the library. He went to investigate and found Ella sniffling near the nonfiction books.

"What's the matter?" he said.
"My dog d-d-died," Ella replied.
And she put her face in her hands and cried.
"Oh dear," murmured Rio, who didn't know what
to say. So he went to get the librarian.

The librarian came over right away.
"Can I help?" she asked Ella.
"No…" Ella gulped back her tears. "My dog
Buster died and I'm going to be sad forever."

"I'm sorry to hear that," said the librarian. "I once had a dog named Sonny. When he died, I thought I'd never stop crying." Ella looked up. "So what happened next?" she said.

"Well," said the librarian, "at first, I didn't want to talk about my dog at all. I felt too sad.

But after a while, I started thinking about some of the funny things Sonny used to do.
Then I felt a little better."

"When he was a puppy, Buster used to wag his tail so hard that he fell over," said Ella, with the tiniest smile. Rio smiled, too.

That afternoon, Mr. Thomas read out the names for the school basketball team. "I don't believe it," Jordan muttered to Rio when the PE teacher had finished speaking. "I'm not on the team." His face fell.

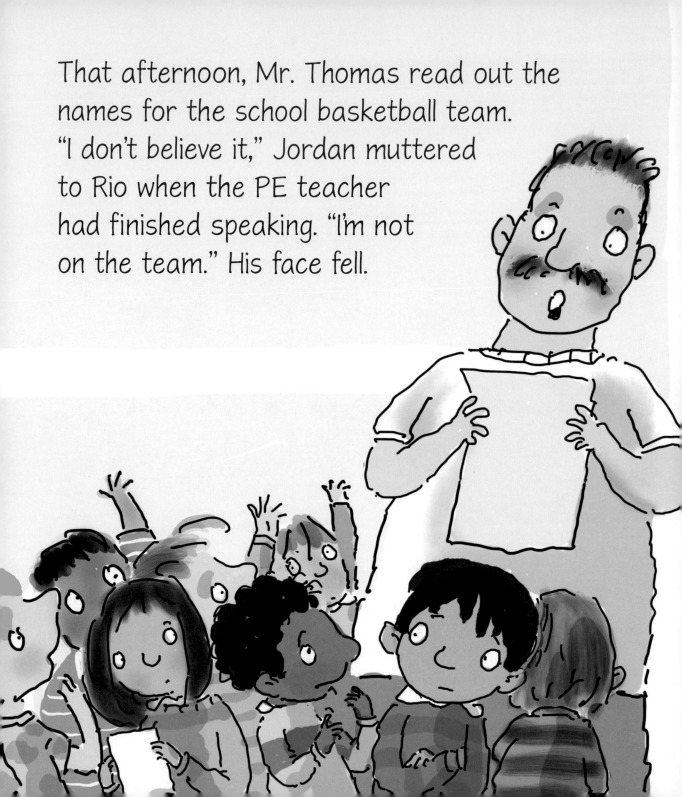

"Awww, Jordan," said Rio. He knew how much his friend wanted to be a basketball player when he grew up. "That's too bad."

"I might as well give up," Jordan said sadly.

Rio hated seeing his friend look so glum.
"*Don't* give up," he said to Jordan.
"Why not?" said Jordan. "If I haven't
been picked, then what's the point?"

"Come on," said Rio. "Why don't we go talk to Mr. Thomas and tell him how interested you are in the team?"

"Okay," grumbled Jordan.

"You're a really good player, Jordan," said Mr. Thomas. "I just need you to work on your dribbling and shooting skills before I can put you on the team. Can you do that?"

Jordan beamed. "Of course!" he said.
"I'm going to start right now."
And he gave Rio a high five.

After school, Rio headed home.
He felt like he'd been cheering people up all day.
But now it was his turn to feel sad. His dad was
working away from home and he really missed him.

"How many days are left now,
Mom?" he asked.

   "Fourteen," said his mom brightly.

   "FOURTEEN?" Rio made a face.

"Cheer up," Mom said. "Dad will be home in just two weeks. That's hardly any time at all." "That's *forever*," said Rio. "Why can't Dad work here, like everyone else's parents?"

"Sorry, honey," said Mom.
"Dad's in construction. So he has to travel
to where the work is. And right now, the bridge
he's building is a long way from home."
Rio knew all this. But he didn't
feel any better.

Thirteen days, twelve days, eleven days…Rio couldn't believe how slowly time was passing. And he still felt sad.

Then he thought of Markus and Ella and Jordan. If he could help them feel happier, why couldn't he do the same for himself?

Rio knew that he couldn't make time go any faster, but he *could* keep himself busy. So he swam, he ran, he read, he hung out with friends, and he played the guitar.

He visited his great-grandma, who told him how his great-grandpa went away during the war. And before he knew it, his dad was home.

"I missed you so much!" said Dad, giving Rio a huge hug.

"I missed you too," said Rio. "I tried not to be too sad while you were away, but I'm *really* happy that you're back."

# NOTES FOR PARENTS AND TEACHERS

The aim of this book is to help children think about their feelings in an enjoyable, interactive way. Encourage kids to have fun pointing out details in the illustrations, making sound effects, and role playing. Here are more ideas for getting the most out of the book:

✱ Encourage children to talk about their own feelings, if they feel comfortable doing so, either while you are reading the book or afterward. Here are some conversation prompts to try:

- When are some times you feel sad? Why?

- How do you stop feeling sad at those times?

- Sometimes people aren't quite sure why they feel sad. What can you do if that happens?

- This story talks about lots of things that people may feel sad about, such as moving to a new school, getting disappointing news, or missing someone. What other reasons can you think of? Now can you think of ways to cheer someone up?

✱ Have children make face masks showing sad expressions. Ask them to explain how these faces show sadness.

* Put on a feelings play! Ask groups of children to act out the different scenarios in the book. The children could use their face masks to show when they are sad in the play.

* Have kids make colorful word clouds. They can start by writing the word *sad*, then add any related words they think of, such as *unhappy* or *tears*. Have children write their words using different colored pens, making the most important words the biggest, and less important words smaller.

* Ask kids to draw pictures or write stories about what sadness feels like to them. Then have them draw pictures or write about times when they feel really happy.

* Invite children to talk about the physical sensations that sadness can bring and where in their bodies they feel sadness. Then discuss things we can do when we're sad, such as talk to people who care about us.

For even more ideas to use with this series, download the free Everyday Feelings Leader's Guide at www.freespirit.com/leader.

*Note:* If a child is continually sad or acts out often due to sadness, seek help from a counselor, psychologist, or other health specialist.

# BOOKS TO SHARE

*A Book of Feelings* by Amanda McCardie,
illustrated by Salvatore Rubbino (Walker, 2016)

*F Is for Feelings* by Goldie Millar and
Lisa A. Berger, illustrated by Hazel Mitchell
(Free Spirit Publishing, 2014)

*The Great Big Book of Feelings*
by Mary Hoffman, illustrated by
Ros Asquith (Frances Lincoln, 2013)

*I'm Not Happy!* by Sue Graves,
illustrated by Desideria Guicciardini
(Free Spirit Publishing, 2011)

*Michael Rosen's Sad Book* by Michael Rosen,
illustrated by Quentin Blake (Candlewick, 2005)

*When I Feel Sad* by Cornelia Maude Spelman, illustrated by
Kathy Parkinson (Albert Whitman & Company, 2002)